The Case of the
Race Against Time

Read all the Jigsaw Jones Mysteries

Don't Miss . . .

And Coming Soon . . .

The Case of the
Race Against Time

by James Preller
illustrated by Jamie Smith
cover illustration by R. W. Alley

A
LITTLE APPLE
PAPERBACK

SCHOLASTIC INC.
New York Toronto London Auckland Sydney
Mexico City New Delhi Hong Kong Buenos Aires

ISBN 0-439-42630-8

12 11 10 9 8 7 6 5 4 3 2 1   3 4 5 6 7 8/0

Printed in the U.S.A.   40
First printing, February 2003

For Nikki Zorian, who cuts my hair at the real Gregory's in Delmar, New York. She does a nice job, if I do say so myself!
—JP

CONTENTS

Chapter One

Late Again

"You're late," my mother snapped.

Four pairs of eyes turned when I walked into the room. Mom, Dad, and Grams sat at the kitchen table, staring at me. Their knives and forks were frozen in midair. It was as if someone had shouted, "Red light!" in a game of Red Light, Green Light. Even our dog, Rags, seemed unhappy.

"Um, sorry," I replied.

"Sorry is not good enough, Jigsaw," my father said. "We expect you to be on time for dinner."

 1

"But I was at Mila's and —"

"But me no buts," he said. "We told you to be home by a quarter to six."

The wall clock read 6:05. Twenty minutes late. I looked around for a rock to crawl under. Too bad there's never one around when you need it.

Grams coughed to fill the silence. "I have a plate warming in the oven for you," she offered. "Go wash your hands and join us."

I was happy to leave the kitchen, even if it meant washing my hands. When I returned to the table, everybody seemed more calm. Rags greeted me with a slobbery lick.

I glanced at all the empty chairs. "Where is everybody?"

My mother sighed. "Daniel and Nick have basketball practice. Hillary is at play rehearsal. And Billy works at the gas station on Thursday nights."

"It feels weird," I said.

"Yes," my father answered. "It sure is quiet."

"Well, I don't like it," my mother complained, rising from her chair. "If I wanted peace and quiet, I'd go live in an igloo. We haven't had a full family dinner since Sunday." She noisily cleared the dirty dishes from the table and put them on the counter with a clatter. Everyone else had already finished eating.

I didn't say a word. When my mom gets angry, it's best to stay far away. Someplace cozy, like Siberia, for example.

Grams helped me load the dishwasher. That was nice. It wasn't her job that night. To be honest, Grams had a good deal at our house. She didn't have any chores. Her only job was to be Grams. And she was pretty darn good at it.

"We missed you at dinner," Grams told me. She slipped me a butterscotch. Then she placed a finger on the tip of my nose and said, "In the future, keep your eye on the time, Jigsaw."

"I would have kept my eye on the time," I said, "but it flew away."

Grams looked puzzled, then smiled. "Oh,

yes. Time flies! I guess you were having fun."

I had been having fun — and I told her all about it. Mila and I were practicing our detective skills by spying on her father. We

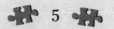

even watched him pick at his toes for ten minutes.

Grams and I were laughing when my mother came into the room.

"Theodore," she said sharply. "Don't you have a test tomorrow? Come on, snap to it. You have studying to do."

Chapter Two

The Gift

Knock, knock. My dad opened the door to my room. I was sitting on the floor, working on a puzzle.

"Can I come in? I'd like to have a little talk with you," he said.

That didn't sound good. Usually, when my dad wanted to have "a little talk," it meant that I'd have "a lot of listen."

He lay down on the carpet beside me. "Tough puzzle, huh?"

I shrugged. "Not so tough. Puzzles are

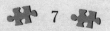

like mysteries. You have to take them one piece at a time."

"How is the detective business going these days?" he asked.

"Slow," I answered. "Mila and I haven't had a case for two weeks. I feel like a hamburger without a bun."

My dad clucked his tongue. He reached into his pocket and pulled out something shiny.

"What's that?" I asked.

"It's a pocket watch," he replied. "This was my father's. *Your* grandfather's."

"Grandpa Jones?"

He nodded. "It's a beauty, isn't it?"

"Why does it have that long chain?" I asked.

He explained that in the old days, lots of men had pocket watches. They clipped the chain to their belt loops and kept the watches in their pants pockets. "That

was before wristwatches became popular," he told me.

"Can I hold it?"

"Actually, Jigsaw, you can *have* it."

"What?!"

"My father gave it to me, and now I'd like to give it to you. That is, if you promise to take extra-special care of it."

I promised.

He brought the watch close to his ear, listening intently. "Takes a licking and keeps on ticking," he murmured. Then he frowned. "Hmmm, the chain is broken. No problem, we can pick up a new chain some time next week. In the meantime, just leave the watch home."

My father placed the pocket watch in my hand.

"Cool. Thanks, Dad!"

"You're welcome, Jigsaw. You deserve it." He gave me a playful punch on the

shoulder. "Now you don't have any reason to be late for dinner. Got it?"

"Got it, Dad."

He stood up the way old people do — with a groan. "Listen, Jigsaw. Maybe you could do something nice for your mother," he suggested. "She's had a hard day."

I told him I'd think of something.

Half an hour later, I found my mother in the living room. She was reading a book, as usual. And as usual, Rags lay on the carpet, warming her feet.

I waited until she looked up. "Here," I said, handing my mother a homemade card. On the cover it read **FOR MOM**. Inside, I

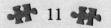

had drawn a huge heart with a crack in it, like old Humpty Dumpty. Three tears dripped out of it. Below the heart I had written SORRY, MOM! I'LL NEVER BE LATE AGAIN. LOVE, JIGSAW.

My mom looked at it for a moment, biting her lip.

She squished me with a hug. Then a tear fell from her eye. "I'm sorry, too," she whispered into my ear.

And I guess that made everything all right.

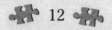

Chapter Three

Room 201

When it comes to haircuts, I'm not picky. Just cut it, stick a Tootsie-pop in my mouth, and I'm a happy camper.

But that was before I met Vladimir.

It started the next day — on a Friday like any other. It was warm out, so my mom let my brother Nick and me ride our bikes to school. Nick is in fifth grade. He's pretty great, most of the time. Except when he calls me Worm or Shorty. Which is all the time.

Go figure.

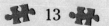

We locked our bikes at the bike racks. Nick said, "Don't forget, Worm. Mom gave me money. We have to go to the barbershop for haircuts after school. Meet me here at three o'clock. And don't be late."

"Got it," I said, "and don't call me Worm."

"Sure thing . . . *Shorty*," he answered.

Oh, brother!

I burst through the main doors and down the hall toward room 201. I couldn't wait to

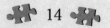 14

show my new pocket watch to my friends. My teacher, Ms. Gleason, was sitting at her desk, looking through some papers. I checked my pocket watch. 8:53. Good, there were still a few minutes before class started.

A bunch of us gathered together on the reading rug, where I proudly showed off my new watch.

"Sweet!" Eddie Becker exclaimed when he saw it. "I bet that's worth a lot of money!"

"Does it really work?" Lucy wondered.

"It takes a licking and keeps on ticking," I told her.

Bobby Solofsky made a sucking sound by running his tongue across his teeth. Just imagine a cow wearing jeans and a T-shirt and you've got the idea.

"Big whoop-de-do," he muttered. "I have a glow-in-the-dark digital watch." He held out his wrist so everyone could see.

No one paid any attention.

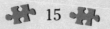 15

So Bobby stormed away. He didn't like being ignored. Like my dad says, jealousy is not a pretty thing.

"Can I hold it?" Bigs Maloney asked. Bigs reached out a hand the size of a garden shovel.

"Um, well, I'm really not even supposed to have it in school today," I explained to Bigs. "This watch is really special and it's my responsibility. . . ."

"I won't break it," Bigs insisted.

Bigs Maloney was the biggest, toughest kid in the whole second grade. He wasn't someone who took no for an answer. Fortunately, Ms. Gleason spoke up. "Okay, boys and girls. Let's get into our seats. Put everything away. It's time to work."

Bigs groaned. I carefully placed the watch in the mesh pocket of my backpack and hung it in my cubby.

Chapter Four
The Nightmare Haircut

Gregory's Barbershop is in a strip of stores a few blocks from school. Everybody goes there. Inside, there are six barber chairs that are always filled. There's Gregory Sr. (he's the dad), Gregory Jr. (he's the son), and Nikki (she's the daughter). I guess you could say that hair is the family business.

A bunch of other people work there, too, cutting hair or cleaning up or answering the phone. I never learned their names.

I always get my haircut from Gregory Sr.,

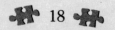

just like my dad. After every haircut he brushes me off, winks, then warns, "Now be careful when you stand up. You might feel a little light-headed."

He says that every time, to every customer. And he always says it with the same cheerful grin and wink.

Go figure.

Nick and I locked our bikes up outside and then dropped our schoolbags near the coatrack by the front door. The girl at the front desk told me that Gregory Sr. had to leave early. "Would you mind getting a haircut from Vladimir?" she asked.

"Vlady-WHO? I mean, sure," I said with a shrug. "Why not?"

"He's a little . . . *new*," the girl explained.

"Whatever," I replied.

Then I saw Vladimir.

He wore superbaggy jeans and a black T-shirt. He had tattoos on both arms — mostly killer snakes, fire-breathing dragons,

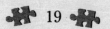

and other creatures from the Forest of Gloom. But it was Vladimir's hair that was the most unusual thing about him. It stood out in strange spikes that bent and flipped in crazy directions.

And, oh, yeah, it came in three colors: blue, green, and red.

"Er, hi," I said.

Vladimir smiled. His eyes twinkled. "So you're my next victim!"

I can't say I loved the sound of that. I followed him to the barber chair.

"Hi, Jigsaw," a voice called. I turned. It was Bigs Maloney. He was already in the chair next to me. Beside Bigs was another face I knew. It was Reginald Pinkerton Armitage III, the richest kid in town. Mila and I worked on a case for him once.

Vladimir jabbed a sharp finger into my shoulder. "You'll need to take off the hat."

"How long have you worked here?" I wondered.

Vladimir smirked. "Oh, about six hours."

"Six hours!"

My hands began to sweat.

"Don't be nervous. I know what I'm doing," Vladimir said. Then he added, "I've been practicing on my dog for years."

"Your dog?!" I exclaimed.

"Yeah, Spike," he replied.

My heart raced faster. I stuttered, "Er, um, maybe this isn't such a good idea. . . . I'm late and I have to . . . er . . ."

A big grin crossed Vladimir's face.

He laughed happily. "I'm joking. What kind of cut would you like?"

"Just a little shorter," I managed to squeak out.

Once I got used to the sight of Vladimir holding a pair of razor-sharp scissors, I relaxed a little. Actually, it seemed like Vladimir knew what he was doing after all. Sitting there, listening to the *clip-snip* of scissors, I let out a yawn. I suddenly felt sleepy. Haircuts do that to me. My eyes grew heavy. My shoulders sagged. And I felt tired, so tired. . . .

I must have fallen asleep. Because I didn't open my eyes until it was too late. The haircut was over. And the damage had been done.

I stared into the mirror, horrified.

My hair looked exactly like Vladimir's. Globs of gooey gel made it stand out in crazy spikes that twisted and turned like spaghetti.

"What did you DO??!!" I screamed.

Vladimir tilted back his head and roared with laughter: "BWAAA-HA-HAAAA!!!"

* * *

"Jigsaw, wake up! We're all done."

A hand shook my shoulder.

"Huh? What?? HELP!" I screamed.

"Easy, easy," the voice soothed. "You were asleep. I think you were having a bad dream."

I blinked myself awake. I looked at myself in the mirror. My hair looked . . . *fine*. Better than fine, actually. Vladimir stood by my side, smiling proudly. "So what do you think? It's a nice haircut, no?"

"It looks great," I admitted. My heart was still pounding from the nightmare. "How long was I asleep?"

"Ten minutes, maybe," Vladimir answered.

I met my brother at the front desk, where he paid for our haircuts. "Nice haircut, Worm," he commented. "Grab your lollipop and let's hit the road."

We walked out to our bicycles. "That was some cool dude who cut your hair," Nick observed.

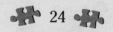 24

"I guess," I said.

"He did a great job," Nick said. "I'm going to ask for him next time."

I climbed onto my bike.

"Hey, Worm," Nick said. "Aren't you forgetting something?"

I stared at him blankly. "Give me a clue."

"Duh, your backpack."

Oh, right. My backpack. I ran inside to get it.

A few minutes later I walked out of Gregory's.

"What's wrong?" Nick asked. "You look like somebody just drowned your pet goldfish."

"My — my backpack," I stammered. "It's gone!"

Chapter Five

An Urgent Message

"Look harder," Nick ordered.

"I already did," I barked. I had left my backpack by the coatrack near the front door. There was a bunch of other bags and backpacks there. But mine was definitely gone.

"Do you think someone stole it?" Nick asked.

I frowned. A thought suddenly popped into my head. "My pocket watch! It was in the mesh pocket of my backpack. Anybody could have seen it."

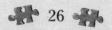

"The pocket watch that Dad gave you?"
Nick asked. "If you lost that watch, Jigsaw,
you'll be grounded for life."

"Yeah, tell me something I don't know," I
glumly replied.

Nick just shook his head. "It's getting
late. We were supposed to come right
home."

"Hold your horses," I pleaded. "I have to
think."

While Nick waited impatiently, I ran
inside Gregory's. I gave the girl at the front
desk my name and phone number. "Please,
please, please call me if you find it," I urged.

She nodded. "We'll take another good
look at closing time. I'm sure it will turn up."

I noticed the appointment calendar on
her desk. It was filled with names and
times. "Is that a list of everyone who had
haircuts at around the same time as me?"

"Yes, I write down every appointment,"
she said.

I borrowed a pad and a sheet of paper. My detective journal was in my backpack, too. That meant double trouble.

I scribbled down the names of everyone who had been in the shop at the same time as me.

At least now I had a list of suspects.

SUSPECTS
Kayla Lewis

Bigs Maloney

Freddy Fenderbank

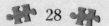

Earl Bartholemew
David Chang
Reginald Pinkerton Armitage III
Gus

Nick opened the door. "Jigsaw, come on!" he shouted. "Do you want to be late again?"

I looked around the waiting room one last time, hoping that my backpack would magically appear. *Poof.* It didn't.

"I'm a dead man," I muttered to Nick as we rode home.

"No," Nick replied. "You're a detective. If anyone can find that backpack, you can."

That cheered me up. A little.

But I knew I'd need help.

The minute I got home, I rushed into my room. I didn't want my mother to see that I was missing a backpack. "Come on, Rags," I told my dog. "We have work to do."

I quickly wrote a note to Mila. I used an alternate word code. My message read:

I your time running we've a case need help is out got new.

It was a simple code. All I did was write my message on a sheet of paper:

I need your help. Time is running out. We've got a new case.

Then I copied it on another scrap of paper, this time skipping every other word.

I your time running we've a case.

Then I went back and did it over again.

Need help is out got new.

Mila was supersmart. She'd figure it out.

I taped the message inside Rags's collar, then made a quick call to Mila. "Don't talk," I whispered into the phone. "Our enemies have ears. Rags is on his way."

Mila coughed three times and hung up. That meant she got the message. I brought Rags to the front door. "Go, boy. Find Mila."

Mila's voice called from down the block, *"Raaaaags! I've got a yummy treat for you!"*

Rags raced off, chasing a snack. My four-footed furball of a dog was just like my friend Joey Pignattano. They'd both do anything for food. And they'd both eat just about anything.

Though, come to think of it, even Rags wouldn't eat a worm for a dollar.

Chapter Six

Nineteen Hours

Mila came over after dinner, around seven o'clock.

"I would have come sooner," she said, "but I had to practice the piano." Mila moved her fingers across the air, playing an imaginary piano.

I guess it beat playing the tuba.

"You practice all the time," I complained. "Don't you know how to play that thing yet?"

Mila rolled her eyes.

We decided to go to my office. It was a

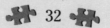

wobbly tree house in my backyard. I poured us both tall glasses of grape juice and we got down to business.

Mila asked me to tell her all about the case — every detail, every fact. She rocked back and forth while she listened, pulling on her long black hair. Next Mila studied the list of suspects.

"Kayla Lewis," Mila noted. "That's Kim's sister. She could have heard about the pocket watch from Kim. We've tangled with her before."

"Yeah, she was in on the necklace robbery," I recalled. "She teamed up with her boyfriend, Buzzy Lennon."

I pointed back to the list. "You already know Bigs Maloney, of course," I said.

Mila nodded. "Bigs seemed to really like your watch."

"Yeah," I agreed. "And he wasn't happy when I didn't let him hold it."

I looked at the list again. "Freddy

Fenderbank. He's my neighbor Wingnut O'Brien's best friend. Those two are like peanut butter and jelly. You never see one without the other."

"Earl Bartholemew," Mila mused. "Why does that name ring a bell?"

"Earl lives across the street from Ralphie Jordan," I replied. "He's a teenager, and teenagers are always trouble. He wears his hair slicked up in the front and short on the sides. He rides a skateboard everywhere he goes."

"And you remember David Chang," I added. "He was in on the robbery when Ralphie's brother sort of 'borrowed' Ralphie's bike without asking."

"That makes him another good suspect," Mila confirmed.

We didn't need to talk about Reginald.

"He's too rich to steal, don't you think?" Mila asked.

I shrugged. "Maybe, maybe not. Reggie

will do just about anything to make friends. We should talk to him. Who knows? He might have seen something."

"I don't know about this Gus guy," Mila said.

"We'll have to track him down," I concluded.

Just then, my dad wandered into the yard. "Hello, Mila. How's the weather up there?"

"Just fine, Mr. Jones!" Mila called down.

"Are you two working on a mystery?"

"Yes —" Mila began.

"NO!" I nearly screamed.

My father looked at me curiously. I fumbled to explain, "Mila means, er, yes *and* no. Sort of. We're just fooling around, kinda."

"Yeah, kinda," Mila added sheepishly.

My father scratched his head. "Okaaaaay," he said. "Well, finish up soon, kiddo. It's your bath night."

Yeesh. This was no time for soap and bubbles. I had a mystery to solve.

As he moved to leave, my father suddenly turned around. "Oh, yes, one more thing, Jigsaw. I have some errands to run tomorrow morning, but I thought we could get you a new chain for that pocket watch. How does three o'clock sound?"

I couldn't speak for a few moments. "Tomorrow?" I asked.

"Yes, three o'clock," he said with a happy grin. "And I know you won't be late now that you've got that pocket watch."

"No, I won't be late," I hollered down. Then I whispered to Mila, "Great, just great. This case gets harder every minute."

Mila checked her watch. "It's almost eight o'clock," she said. "That means we only have about nineteen hours to find your backpack."

I took notes on a clean sheet of paper:

CASE: The Race Against Time.
CLIENT: Me!

I had to find that backpack, or else.

"Nineteen hours," I grumbled. "Time sure flies when you're having a bad day."

Chapter Seven

From Bad to Worse

After my bath, my luck went from bad to worse. First my sister, Hillary, talked on the phone forever. She whispered and giggled and exclaimed, "Oh, my gosh! Oh, my gosh!"

I told her I was on a case. I had suspects to call. I demanded to use the phone.

Hillary only paused to hiss me away.

The second Hillary hung up — finally! — the phone rang. It was my brother Billy's new girlfriend, Rain. That was her real name! I wondered if her sisters were named Fog and Partly Cloudy. Anyway, she sounded like a *drip* to me. They talked forever while I stood by politely waiting — though I did groan a lot. Maybe the phrase "C'mon already!" passed my lips a few dozen times.

Billy threw a smelly sock at me.

It hit me right in the eye.

I did manage to get in one phone call before bedtime.

"Armitage residence," the voice answered. "Reginald speaking."

"Reggie? It's Jigsaw."

Reggie didn't remember seeing anything strange at the barbershop, but he did know something about Gus. "He's our family chauffeur," he told me.

"Your what?"

"Our driver," Reginald explained.

"Oh," I answered. "Our driver's name is Mom."

"You're funny, Jones." Reginald chuckled.

"Yeah, a laugh riot," I murmured. I waited a few ticks before asking, "This Gus, do you think he's the kind of guy who might steal?"

"Never," Reginald claimed. "Gus is like a member of our family. Besides, I would have seen him with the backpack, wouldn't I?"

Made sense to me.

Then it was time for my reading and for

bed. See, my teacher, Ms. Gleason, was real big on reading. And my parents teamed up with her. I had to read half an hour every night. I read *Because of Winn-Dixie* by Kate Dicamillo. It was a little too hard for me, but my mother helped me with it. That's the thing with reading. Even when you're miserable, a good book can take you away to another place.

And that's where I wanted to be.

Anywhere but here.

Still, I couldn't stop thinking about time. *Ticktock*. I glanced at my bedroom clock (it glowed in the dark). It read 9:36. Time went on forever, but for some reason, I was running out of it.

Hickery, dickery, dock. The mouse ran up the clock.

Only seventeen hours and twenty-four minutes left until —

Correction: Make that seventeen hours and twenty-three minutes.

Yeesh.

I hated to go to bed. I didn't have time for sleep. I still had so much to do. I lay my head on the pillow and decided that sleep was a waste of time.

Then I fell asleep. Yeesh.

Chapter Eight

Brrriiinnnggg!

I woke up at exactly 7:13 the next morning and quickly did the math. My dad was taking me to fix the watch at 3:00. I had less than eight hours to solve the case — and I was still in my pajamas.

The phone rang during my second bowl of Rice Krispies.

My mother answered. "It's Gregory's Barbershop," she said. "It's someone named . . . *Vladimir*."

She looked at me with her eyebrows raised in a question. My face gave no answers.

She hovered nearby until I covered the phone with my hand. "It's business, Mom. I need to talk in private."

My mother sighed loudly and walked into the kitchen.

"This is Jigsaw," I whispered into the receiver.

"Jigsaw, this is Vladimir. Do you remember me?"

"Is this Vladimir the barber, or Vladimir the baseball player?"

"Huh?"

"Just kidding," I cracked. "Yeah, sure, I remember."

"I heard you lost a backpack yesterday," Vladimir said. "Well, we looked all over this morning and I found one hidden behind a large potted plant."

"You did?"

I wondered how it could have gotten there.

"Are you sure it's mine?" I asked. "Is my detective journal inside?"

"Let me check," Vladimir answered. He came back to the phone a minute later. "Sorry, Jigsaw. You'll have to come down. It's store policy never to look inside anyone's stuff," he told me. "Dem's da rules."

"Tell me this," I asked, "is it a black Jansport with a blue label?"

Vladimir told me that it was.

"Can you see a silver pocket watch in the outside mesh pocket?"

"Nope, no watch," Vladimir replied. He paused, then added, "There's a key ring attached to the zipper . . . with a picture of NASCAR driver Jeff Gordon."

My heart sank. It wasn't my backpack after all.

But what if . . . ?

My brain started racing, and I knew one thing: I *had* to get a look inside that backpack even if it meant stretching the truth so thin it looked like tracing paper. "Yes," I told Vladimir. "That's the one. I'll be there as quick as I can."

Fifteen minutes later Mila and I were racing on our bicycles. It was 9:30 and we only had five and a half hours left to solve the case. My blood was pumping with excitement. Finally, we were going to get a look at our first clue.

Mila had already checked on most of the

suspects. Nothing turned up. There was no answer at the Fenderbanks' house and she kept getting busy signals at David Chang's.

"Tell me again," Mila said as we parked our bikes. "Why are you so interested in picking up the wrong backpack?"

"It's just a hunch," I said. "But I'm thinking that somebody might have taken my backpack by mistake."

Mila nodded. "Could be. They were both black. I guess they looked about the same. If the person was in a hurry . . . but . . ."

"But what?" I asked.

"But wouldn't the person have figured it out by now?" Mila said. "I mean, after they got home?"

"Today is Saturday. You know that no kid does schoolwork on the weekends. Anyway," I continued, "it's our only hope."

We leaned our bikes up against the streetlight, and into Gregory's Barbershop we went.

Chapter Nine
Find Freddy

Vladimir tossed the backpack into my arms. "Here you go, Jigsaw!"

Mila stood staring at his blue, green, and red hair. It looked like it had been cut by a lawn mower and combed by a hurricane. "Awesome hair," she observed.

"Thanks," Vladimir replied. "I'll give you a haircut just like it any time you want."

"No, thanks," Mila replied. "It wouldn't match my pink sneakers."

I quickly zipped open the backpack. Inside was a lunch box, a spelling book,

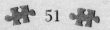 51

and a homework folder. Neatly lettered on each one was the name FREDDY FENDERBANK.

This was the clue we needed!

Still, I looked at Vladimir and pretended to be disappointed. "Rats. Wrong back-pack."

"Bummer," Vladimir groaned.

"That's okay," I said with a smile. "Anyway, thanks again. I have to run. Time flies, you know!"

We pushed open the door and raced to our bikes.

Freddy Fenderbank lived on Abbey Road near my friend Stringbean Noonan. It was a long, uphill ride. It was 10:36 A.M.

I knocked on the door.

No one answered.

I rang the bell.

No one answered all over again.

Mila and I sat on the front stoop, heads in our hands. "What do we do now?" I wondered.

"We could stay here and wait," Mila offered.

"We only have a little more than four hours left!" I said. "I *can't* sit around twiddling my thumbs."

Suddenly Mila snapped her fingers. "Wingnut O'Brien! He's best friends with Freddy. Maybe Wingnut knows where we can find him."

Once again, we climbed on our bicycles and raced off. This time, we were headed back to my neighborhood. My leg muscles ached. My back hurt. Sweat poured down my face. We kept on pedaling even though I wanted to stop and rest. Faster and faster.

There was no car in Wingnut O'Brien's driveway. But loud music throbbed from behind the front door. That is, if you could call it music. It sounded more like a car wreck. We pounded on the door for a full minute. Finally, Wingnut's teenage brother, Jake, opened the door. Everyone called him

Jake the Snake because he loved snakes. I mean, he really, really *loved* snakes.

Go figure.

"What do you pipsqueaks want?" Jake snarled. "No one's home."

We told him we were looking for Wingnut. Jake told us to look somewhere else. "He left with Freddy about ten minutes ago," Jake said.

"Ten minutes ago!" I exclaimed.

"Where did they go?" Mila asked.

"Out," Jake explained.

He started to shut the door. I blocked it

with my foot. "Did they take bikes? Walk? Go by car?"

"Bikesss," Jake hissed. "Now go away or I'll bring out my boa constrictor."

He slammed the door shut.

"What a nice guy," Mila muttered. "NOT!"

"What time is it now?" I asked.

Mila checked her wristwatch. "Eleven o'clock sharp."

That left us with less than four hours to find Freddy Fenderbank. Or else.

I hopped on my bike. "Let's go," I told Mila.

"Where?" Mila asked.

"I don't know!" I nearly screamed. "Somewhere! Anywhere! I have to get that backpack or I'm toast."

"Calm down," Mila ordered. She grabbed my handlebars. "There has to be a better way."

"Yeah, what's that?" I snapped.

Mila gave a sly grin.

"Search party."

Chapter Ten

The Search Party

Mila and I called everyone we knew from school. Some kids were home. Some weren't. But everybody we talked to wanted to help. We told them all to meet at my tree house. They came on bikes, on Rollerblades, on skateboards. Ralphie Jordan and Danika Starling brought extra sets of walkie-talkies. Even Bigs Maloney came along.

By noon, we were ready to roll.

Mila took charge. She and I stood high in my tree house, while everyone gathered on

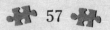

the grass below. There was Ralphie, Bigs, Danika, Kim, Stringbean, Joey, and Geetha. That made nine of us altogether.

"Look at that," Mila said. "You have a lot of friends, Jigsaw."

And you know what? For that moment, looking at everyone in my backyard, I felt like the luckiest guy on earth. For one minute, at least, I didn't worry about the pocket watch or getting in trouble with my

dad. I had friends, lots of them. And they all wanted to help me.

Mila studied a map of the town. She circled spots on the map with a red marker.

I held up a photograph of Freddy Fenderbank. It was taken at last year's camping trip at Enchanted Lake. I'll say this: The kid sure had a lot of freckles. Yeesh.

"Here's your mission," Mila stated, like a sheriff leading a posse. "Find Freddy Fenderbank. We have reason to believe that Freddy has Jigsaw's backpack." Mila paused to check her watch. "We have less than three hours."

Then she barked out orders like a general.

"Bigs, Ralphie!" Mila shouted, "You guys take the playground at school. Be sure to check Hodges Field and the basketball courts."

"Check," Bigs answered.

"Danika, Geetha, and I will go to Lincoln Park on Rollerblades," Mila stated.

She pointed down to Joey and Stringbean. "Stringbean, you know Freddy's neighborhood the best. Cruise around on your bike. Check every street you can find."

"Check," Stringbean replied.

"Joey, go on your skateboard into town," Mila commanded. "Be sure to check all the stores on Waverly Avenue — especially Grandma's Bakery."

Joey smiled happily. "You got it, Mila."

"But Joey," Mila said, "don't stop to eat anything."

We all laughed at that.

"What about me?" Kim asked.

Mila circled a spot on the map. "You're at the library, Kim."

"Check."

"Okay, guys," Mila shouted. "Be sure to

bring your walkie-talkies or money for the pay phone. Jigsaw will be waiting here."

"No way," I interrupted. "Mysteries don't get solved by sitting around. I'll keep a walkie-talkie with me. We can all meet back here at five minutes before three o'clock."

Mila nodded in agreement. She called down, "Are . . . you . . . ready?"

"YES!" everyone shouted.

And off they scattered to find Freddy Fenderbank.

I was just about to leave on my bike when a surprise visitor showed up.

It was Reginald Pinkerton Armitage III. He was dressed in neat khakis and wore a tidy bow tie over a white button-down shirt.

"Jigsaw," he said, "I understand you may be in need of some assistance."

"Huh?" I answered.

Reginald cleared his throat. "I hear you need some help."

I told him all about it.

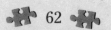

Reginald nodded grimly. He pulled a cell phone from his back pocket. "Gus," he spoke into the phone. "I need you immediately. Bring the limo."

"Wow, thanks, Reggie," I said, giving him a pat on the back.

With his right pinky, Reginald pushed a pair of round eyeglasses from the tip of his nose closer to his face. "Jones," he said, "you once helped me when I was new in town without a friend in the world. An Armitage never forgets a favor."

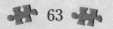

Chapter Eleven

Ticktock

I staked out Freddy Fenderbank's house. If he came home, I wanted to be there waiting for him. Reginald had lent me his wristwatch. I checked it every ten minutes. Then every five minutes.

Nothing.

Every once in a while somebody would call on the walkie-talkie. The message was always the same. No sign of Freddy Fenderbank. It felt like we were looking for an invisible boy.

Freddy's garage door had a row of small

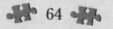

windows. I pulled myself up and peered into the shadows. I noticed two bicycles leaning against a wall. I knew whose bikes they were. Freddy's and Wingnut's. My heart sank. There was no car in the drive-way. They must have gone somewhere in the car with Freddy's mother.

But where?

At 2:17, Mila called. "Jigsaw, I'm at the pay phone outside Huck's Hardware. Listen, I just met a kid who says that

Freddy has been talking about going to Hoffberg's Playland all week long."

"Hoffberg's?" I blurted. "That's ten minutes away by car! We can never get there and back by three o'clock."

"It's a long shot, but it's the best tip we've gotten yet. Any other news?"

"Only the bad kind," I replied. Then I remembered. "Reginald stopped by. He has a car. Maybe there's still a chance."

"I'm on it," Mila said crisply. "Do you have his phone number?"

"Yes, it's in my —" My voice trailed off. Yes, I had Reginald's phone number. It was in my detective journal. That was in my backpack.

"I'll figure out something," Mila said. "Over and out."

"Over and out," I echoed. Then I jumped on my bike and hurried home.

At exactly 2:32, my dad pulled into the driveway. At the same moment I rode up on my bike, panting and nervous. "Let's go, kiddo!" he called to me happily. "Klonsky's Jewelers or bust!"

I groaned, "Is it time already?"

My father frowned. "Excuse me, Jigsaw? That's not the response I expected. Don't you *want* to go?"

I could see the disappointment in his face. This pocket watch meant a lot to him. His father had given it to him. He had given it to me.

"Sorry, Dad," I mumbled. "I'll be ready in a second. Just let me go to the bathroom first. I've got to, um, you know."

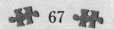

"Gotcha," he answered. "I'll wait in the car."

I did everything I could think of to buy more time. I slowly brushed my teeth. I flossed. I combed my hair. I grabbed a snack from the kitchen. All the while, I watched through the windows for any sign of somebody with a backpack.

No one came.

Beep, beep. BEEP!

I couldn't stall any longer.

I was closing my front door when, suddenly, Bigs Maloney and Ralphie Jordan raced along my sidewalk on their bikes. I held out my arms in question. "Well?"

Ralphie shook his head from side to side. Bigs frowned and gave me the thumbs-down sign.

I walked slowly to the car with my head down.

More kids showed up. Danika and Geetha on Rollerblades. Stringbean, Joey, and Kim. None of them had my backpack.

And I still hadn't heard from Mila.

"That's quite a crowd," my father observed. "What are all your friends doing here?"

I shrugged. "Beats me."

"Do you have the watch?" my father asked.

I patted an empty pocket.

My father took that as a yes.

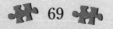

I felt bad, but there was still hope. Maybe Mila could find Reggie. Maybe together they could still find Freddy and meet me at the jewelers before three. I couldn't give up now. Not with Mila out there doing everything she could to help me.

I'd have to play this out to the very end.

Chapter Twelve

Time's Up

There was a digital clock on the dashboard of my dad's car. I couldn't take my eyes off it. At 2:53, we pulled into the parking lot at Klonsky's Jewelers.

I bent down to tie my shoe at the heavy front door. It didn't exactly need tying, but I needed to steal every second I could get. I scanned the sidewalks. I looked right, then left. No sign of Mila or Reggie. I tied the other shoe.

"I think they're tight enough," my dad commented.

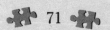 71

Klonsky's was a clean, well-lit store, with long rows of glass cases. A few ladies and a thin, gray-haired man stood behind them. They opened the cases with little keys. They talked quietly with customers. They smiled and nodded and fussed over diamonds and pearls.

We waited until the older man was finished with his customer. "May I help you?" he asked us.

My father explained why we were there.

"Excellent," said the jeweler. He held out an open palm. It was old and wrinkled but surprisingly large. "If I may see the watch in question?" he asked.

And for that one second — that sliver of a moment — time seemed to stand still. Frozen at exactly 2:59. I stood there, speechless. I couldn't move.

Then I felt a bump behind me. A hand on my shoulder.

"Jigsaw? Jigsaw Jones?"

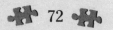

I turned to see Reginald Pinkerton Armitage III. Mila stood behind him. She ran a finger across her nose. It was our secret signal. The smile on her face told me everything I needed to know.

They had the watch.

"What in the world are you doing here?" Reginald asked in fake surprise. He swiftly reached out to shake my hand, pumping it up and down like a seesaw.

When he was done, I felt the heavy silver watch in my hand. Reggie had secretly slipped it to me during the handshake.

We had won the race!

Just in the nick of time.

Together, my father and I picked out a cool-looking chain. "I'm proud of you, son," my father said. "I know that you'll take great care of that pocket watch."

"I will," I promised. "It will never leave my sight."

The chain was attached to my belt loop

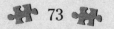

and the watch was safely tucked into my pocket. I pulled it out. "It's exactly three-fifteen," I announced. "A good time for a slice of pizza, don't you think?"

My father laughed. "Jigsaw, you always think it's a good time for pizza."

Later that afternoon Reggie and I met up at Mila's house. I made Mila and Reggie tell me everything that had happened while I was with my dad. Then I asked them to tell me again — and again. It turned out that Reginald had come through for us, big time.

Mila had managed to reach Reggie on his cell phone. Reggie and Gus picked her up and drove to Hoffberg's. It's a small amusement park, but it wasn't easy finding Freddy. They tried the whiplash ride, the Ferris wheel, the house of mirrors. Finally, they found Freddy and Wingnut next to the bumper cars, stuffing cotton candy into their faces.

"It took some explaining to Freddy's mother," Mila said, "but I told her it was a super-emergency. She let Gus drive us all to Freddy's house so we could pick up the backpack."

"Naturally, that's not the end of the story," Reggie added. "Once we got the backpack, Gus drove us to your house, but we were too late. It seemed we had just missed you."

"Your mother told us that you were at Klonsky's Jewelers," Mila said.

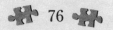

"And that's that," Reggie said, smiling broadly.

"Mila, Reggie, you two are great friends," I said.

Mila smiled back at me.

"Yes," she answered. "And we're pretty good detectives, too."

I reached into my pocket to check the time. 6:05. "Uh-oh!" I said. "I'm late for dinner!"

And off I ran.

Some races, I guess, never end.

About the Author

James Preller often draws upon his own life as a basis for his Jigsaw Jones books. Like Jigsaw, James Preller has a slobbering, sock-eating dog. Like Jigsaw, James was the youngest in a large family. His older brothers called him Worm and worse — yeesh! And so do Jigsaw's!

James and Jigsaw both love jigsaw puzzles, baseball, grape juice, and mysteries! But even though Jigsaw and James have so much in common, they are not the same person.

Unlike Jigsaw, James Preller is the author of more than 80 books for children, including *The Big Book of Picture-Book Authors & Illustrators, Wake Me in Spring, Hiccups for Elephant,* and *Cardinal & Sunflower.* He lives outside of Albany, New York, in a town called Glenmont, with his wife, Lisa, three kids — Nicholas, Gavin, and Maggie — his cat, Blue, and his dog, Seamus.

Here's a sneak peek at the next

A JIGSAW JONES MYSTERY

#21 The Case of the Rainy Day Mystery

Joey Pignattano came over after dinner. In the pouring rain.

And dripped water from his nose to his toes.

"I'm starving," he moaned. Joey swayed from side to side, as if dizzy with hunger.

I led him downstairs. "Okay, turn around and close your eyes," I ordered. I placed a blindfold around his head.

"But I can't see," Joey protested.

"That's the idea," I explained. "Only Mila and I know our secret hiding place."

I crept behind the washing machine and pulled out a box. It was labeled:

KEEP OUT, AND THAT MEANS YOU!

It was where we kept our detective supplies. Walkie-talkies, fingerprint kits, disguises, magnifying glass, rearview sunglasses — that kind of stuff. It was also where I stashed Joey's Twinkies.

"Okay, you can look now," I told Joey.

He pounced like he hadn't eaten in six weeks. It was exactly one hour after dinnertime.

"That's enough," I said after watching him snarf down two Twinkies.

A sad look came into Joey's eyes when I pried the Twinkie box from his grasp. Then Joey cheered up when he saw my detective supplies. He tried on a green wig and fake mustache. Joey put on a trench coat and deerstalker cap. He played with my decoder ring, fiddled with my walkie-talkie, and studied a grape juice stain with a magnifying glass.

"Being a detective must be cool," he said.

"It's a living," I replied with a shrug.

And then I had an idea.

"Joey, are you free on Monday after school?"

"Yeah, why?" he asked.

I told him about my visit with Lucy Hiller. It felt good to talk about the case. Normally, I had Mila for that. Joey was the next-best thing, I guess.

"I have to spy on Bigs Maloney," I said. "The problem is, I have a dentist appointment after school on Monday.

"This case might take a lot of work," I continued. "Following Bigs will be tricky. And Mila is too sick to help. So how'd you like to be my right-hand man?"

"I'd love to, Jigsaw," Joey said. "But I can't."

"Why not?" I asked.

"I'm a lefty."

"So?"

Joey answered, "You said you need a right-hand man."

"I mean that I need a *helper*," I said. "Not a righty."

Joey, as usual, was confused. "So why didn't you say so in the first place?" he asked.

"I thought I did."

Joey shook his head. "Nuh-uh."

We made a deal. I'd hold on to Joey's Twinkies (there were eight left), and he would work with me for free.

"What do you want me to do?" Joey wondered.

I told Joey that I needed him to follow Bigs after school on Monday.

"Be observant," I said.

"Ob-ser-who?"

"Observant," I repeated. "It means 'to look at things closely.'"

Joey nodded as if he understood. I had my doubts.

"Keep your eyes open," I said. "See where he goes, watch what he does. That's it. Just put a tail on Bigs Maloney."

Joey nodded solemnly. "Put a tail on Bigs Maloney."

I stopped Joey on the way upstairs. "Hand it over," I ordered.

"Huh?"

"The Twinkie you slipped in your pocket when you thought I wasn't looking," I said. "Hand it over."

Joey groaned. "Wow, you really are obser-ver-er-er-rer."

"I'm a detective, Joey," I answered. "It's part of the job."

Creepy, weird, wacky, and funny things happen to the Bailey School Kids!™ Collect and read them all!

The Adventures of
THE BAILEY SCHOOL KIDS®

Available wherever you buy books, or use this order form

Scholastic Inc., P.O. Box 7502, Jefferson City, MO 65102

Please send me the books I have checked above. I am enclosing $_____ (please add $2.00 to cover shipping and handling). Send check or money order — no cash or C.O.D.s please.

Name _Salvador_____

Address _____

City_____ State/Zip _____

Please allow four to six weeks for delivery. Offer good in the U.S. only. Sorry, mail orders are not available to residents of Canada. Prices subject to change.   BSK801